This Journal Belongs To

BLACK
HISTORY
MONTH

BLACK
HISTORY
MONTH

BLACK
HISTORY
MONTH

BLACK
HISTORY
MONTH

BLACK
HISTORY
MONTH

BLACK
HISTORY
MONTH

BLACK HISTORY MONTH

BLACK
HISTORY
MONTH

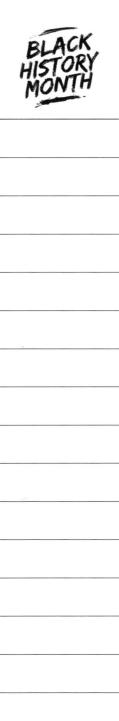

BLACK HISTORY MONTH

BLACK HISTORY MONTH

BLACK HISTORY MONTH

BLACK
HISTORY
MONTH

BLACK
HISTORY
MONTH

BLACK
HISTORY
MONTH

BLACK
HISTORY
MONTH

BLACK
HISTORY
MONTH

BLACK HISTORY MONTH

BLACK HISTORY MONTH

BLACK HISTORY MONTH

BLACK HISTORY MONTH

BLACK HISTORY MONTH

BLACK HISTORY MONTH

Made in the USA
Monee, IL
15 February 2022